Jamie Is Jamie

A Book About Being Yourself and Playing Your Way

Afsaneh Moradian

Illustrated by Maria Bogade

free spirit
PUBLISHING®

Library of Congress Cataloging-in-Publication Data
Names: Moradian, Afsaneh, author. | Bogade, Maria, illustrator.
Title: Jamie is Jamie : a book about being yourself and playing your way / Afsaneh Moradian ; illustrated by Maria Bogade.
Description: Minneapolis, MN : Free Spirit Publishing Inc., [2018] | Summary: Jamie is excited about making friends at a new school, but after playing with dolls and action figures, trying ballet and fixing a toy car, his classmates wonder if Jamie is a girl or a boy. Includes tips for adults. | Identifiers: LCCN 2017033493 (print) | LCCN 2017044573 (ebook) | ISBN 9781631982910 (Web PDF) | ISBN 9781631982927 (ePub) | ISBN 9781631981395 (hardcover) | ISBN 1631981390 (hardcover)
Subjects: | CYAC: Play—Fiction. | Gender identity—Fiction. | Schools—Fiction. | Moving, Household—Fiction.
Classification: LCC PZ7.1.M66825 (ebook) | LCC PZ7.1.M66825 Jam 2018 (print) | DDC [E]—dc23
LC record available at https://lccn.loc.gov/2017033493

Free Spirit Publishing does not have control over or assume responsibility for author or third-party websites and their content.

Reading Level Grade 2; Interest Level Ages 4–8;
Fountas & Pinnell Guided Reading Level K

Edited by Brian Farrey-Latz
Cover and interior design by Shannon Pourciau

10 9 8 7 6 5 4 3 2 1
Printed in China
R18860118

Free Spirit Publishing Inc.
6325 Sandburg Road, Suite 100
Minneapolis, MN 55427-3674
(612) 338-2068
help4kids@freespirit.com
www.freespirit.com

FSC
www.fsc.org
MIX
Paper from
responsible sources
FSC® C101537

Free Spirit offers competitive pricing.
Contact edsales@freespirit.com for pricing information on multiple quantity purchases.

Next, Jamie saw a girl looking in the mirror and posing.
"What are you doing?" asked Jamie.

"I am a ballerina," explained Alicia. "I'm practicing ballet."

"Can I try?" wondered Jamie.

"You have to wear a leotard, a frilly tutu, tights, and special dance shoes to do a pirouette like this."

"Are you strong enough?" replied Joey.

Jamie picked up the wheels, pushed them back into place, and vroomed the car back over to Joey.

"Wow, thanks!" said Joey.

A group of boys were racing cars on the floor. Jamie noticed that the back wheels had popped off one of the cars. A boy named Joey was having trouble putting them back on.

"Can I help?" asked Jamie.

At school the next day, Jamie joined the other kids in free play.

There was so much to do—unpack boxes of toys and clothes and explore the yard outside. Most of all, Jamie was excited to start school and make new friends.

Jamie had just moved to a
new home and neighborhood.

For Roya

Jamie watched as Alicia twirled around. Then Jamie did a perfect pirouette in pants and sneakers. Alicia was surprised.

Jamie heard a baby doll crying and went to see what was wrong.
Cynthia was having trouble. "I can't get her to stop crying."

Jamie held up the baby
doll's head while she
drank . . .

. . . and gently patted her back until she burped. "You did that just like my mommy," Cynthia said.

Next, Jamie went over to a boy playing alone with action figures. "Can I play?" asked Jamie.

"Are you a boy? Only boys can play with action figures," replied Xavier.

"I'm Jamie," answered Jamie, picking up a superhero figure. "We're being attacked by a giant purple Hargermonger!"

Xavier grabbed two superhero figures and fought off the villain with Jamie.

For the rest of free play, Jamie joined a pair of girls doing somersaults, told jokes to some kids until they fell on the floor laughing, finished a dinosaur puzzle with a couple of boys, and played chef in the toy kitchen.

Jamie's mommy was the first parent to arrive at pickup time. Leaving the classroom, Jamie waved goodbye to the other kids.

Alicia said, "Jamie is so graceful. She should be a ballerina one day."

"What? Jamie is a boy," replied Joey. "He fixed my car so fast. He's gonna be a mechanic."

Cynthia said, "Jamie is a great mommy. She knew just how to take care of my baby doll."

Xavier was confused. "Wait a minute . . .
Is Jamie a boy or a girl?"

"I don't know," said Alicia, "but I can't wait to play with Jamie tomorrow. That was a lot of fun!"

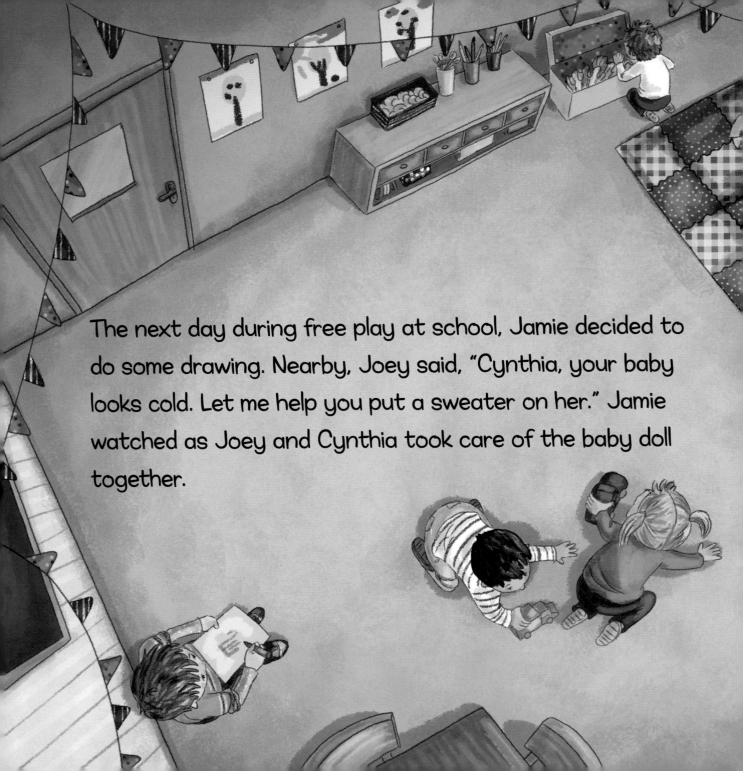

The next day during free play at school, Jamie decided to do some drawing. Nearby, Joey said, "Cynthia, your baby looks cold. Let me help you put a sweater on her." Jamie watched as Joey and Cynthia took care of the baby doll together.

Then, Jamie noticed Alicia using the action figures to teach Xavier different ballet positions. They both made the action figures dance to fight the villain.

"Jamie, come play action figures with us," said Xavier.

"Sure!" Jamie crouched down next to them and whispered, "What's the plan?"

And Jamie was happy because everyone was playing exactly what they wanted to play.

Tips for Teachers, Parents, and Caregivers

As adults, we want to teach children about the world around them and help them learn appropriate and positive behavior. However, children thrive when given time to think and act for themselves. Through play, children learn how to interact with one another, work together, resolve conflicts, and become social beings. Here are some tips to make playtime learning time:

Let children play freely. Children begin to play by copying the world around them. If a boy wants to play house and be the "mommy," or a girl wants to be the "daddy," this is not an indication of who the child will grow to be as an adult. Children copy what they know and what they see. Role play is a common and important aspect of playtime, and allowing children to make their own decisions during play helps them build confidence.

Keep in mind that toys have no gender. Encouraging children to play with any toy they choose enables them to

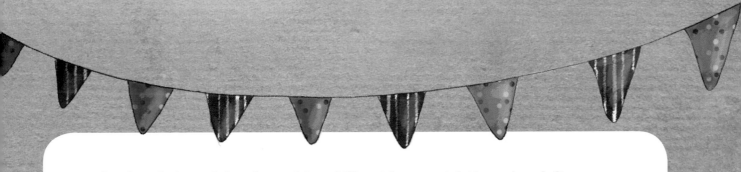

develop their social and cognitive skills without restrictions. As adults, we want to teach our children that the world is open to them and that they can dream and aspire to be whatever they want in the future. So if a boy wants to walk around in high heels and a girl wants to paint a beard on her chin, it's all part of their development.

Let children try to work out their differences on their own. It's tempting to step in to try to organize games or solve small disputes. But when we do this, we deprive children of the chance to use their words and to react to children who think differently or want to do things differently. If two friends don't want to play the same game, watch from afar and see if they can figure out a compromise on their own before rushing in to solve the problem. Of course, there are times when adults need to step in to help children resolve conflicts—especially if the children have become physical or are too frustrated to talk. But first, give them the chance to explore their feelings and to find constructive ways to express those feelings on their own.

Provide children with creative playing materials.
Children who are given the chance to play freely with a variety of materials learn to think creatively and use their imaginations. For example, a child might decide that building blocks can be used to build towers and cities one day, then decide that the blocks are guests at a tea party the next day. There is no "correct" way to play

with a toy. The best way to play is creatively. If no one will be hurt and nothing will be broken, let children enter their own worlds and imagine their toys to be something other than the toy's original purpose. This often leads to children interacting with others and the world around them in ways that help them relate better.

Talk with children about play. We need to have conversations about play with children. Talking helps negate outdated ideas about how kids can play or about what girls can do and what boys can do. Talking also assures children that playtime is truly their time and that they have a say in how it's spent. This book offers a great opportunity to ask questions of children: Is there anything they feel they can't play or don't want to play? Why or why not? Would they want to try new games like Jamie does? By finding out what children are thinking, we can begin a conversation that will help open their minds and will expand upon our own ideas of gender and creative play as well.

About the Author

Afsaneh Moradian has loved writing stories, poetry, and plays since childhood. After receiving her master's in education, she took her love of writing into the classroom, where she began teaching children how to channel their creativity. Her passion for teaching has lasted for over 15 years. Afsaneh now guides students and teachers (and her young daughter) in the art of writing. She lives in New York City.

About the Illustrator

Maria Bogade is an illustrator and author with a background in animation. She loves creating illustrations with a strong narrative—colorful and beautifully composed to entertain children and adults alike. Her work is internationally published and is also found on greeting cards and other products, such as chocolate. With her three children and spouse, Maria lives in a tiny village in southern Germany where fox and hare bid each other goodnight.

More Great Books from Free Spirit

Zach Rules Series

by William Mulcahy, illustrated by Darren McKee

Zach struggles with social issues like getting along, persevering, handling frustrations, making mistakes, dealing with bullying, and other everyday problems typical of young kids. Each book in the Zach Rules series presents a single, simple storyline involving one such problem. As each story develops, Zach and readers learn straightforward tools for coping with their struggles and building stronger relationships now and in the future.
Each book: 32–36 pp., color illust., HC, 8¼" x 8¼", ages 5–8.

Interested in purchasing multiple quantities and receiving volume discounts?
Contact edsales@freespirit.com or call 1.800.735.7323 and ask for Education Sales.

Many Free Spirit authors are available for speaking engagements, workshops, and keynotes.
Contact speakers@freespirit.com or call 1.800.735.7323.

For pricing information, to place an order, or to request a free catalog, contact:

free spirit PUBLISHING®

6325 Sandburg Road • Suite 100 • Minneapolis, MN 55427-3674
toll-free 800.735.7323 • local 612.338.2068 • fax 612.337.5050
help4kids@freespirit.com • www.freespirit.com